Farm Friends

Written and illustrated by

Tony Coleman

Published in 2019
by Jacek M. Pawlowski

ISBN: 978-1-9160256-9-1

This book is dedicated to Sharon,my wife,
who simply said 'You can do it'.
My children: Bailey, Tyler and Skye, who always had bedtime stories, with an extra mention to Skye who once said at a pond: 'I want to feed the big ducks', which put the idea in my head, because they were geese.
And to my friend Jacek, who helped with this project.

Lastly to everyone of you who are about to read this to a child.
I hope this short story provides part of some long memories.

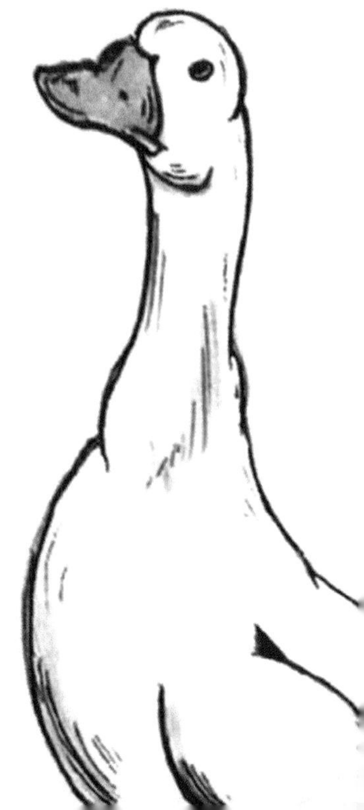

Hey Denize
I hope you gets lots of
Enjoyment from this book.
All the best

11th May 2019.

A duck,
a rabbit, a goose
and a hare.

Lived on a farm
in the country somewhere.

The duck and the rabbit
were the best of mates.
They shared everything,
even dinner plates.

The goose and the hare
were just as buddy.
Playing on the farm
and getting muddy.

One day the rabbit
was having a walk.
He came across goose
and decided to talk.

“You must be duck’s dad
you’re like him, but bigger.”
The goose had a smile
and started to snigger.

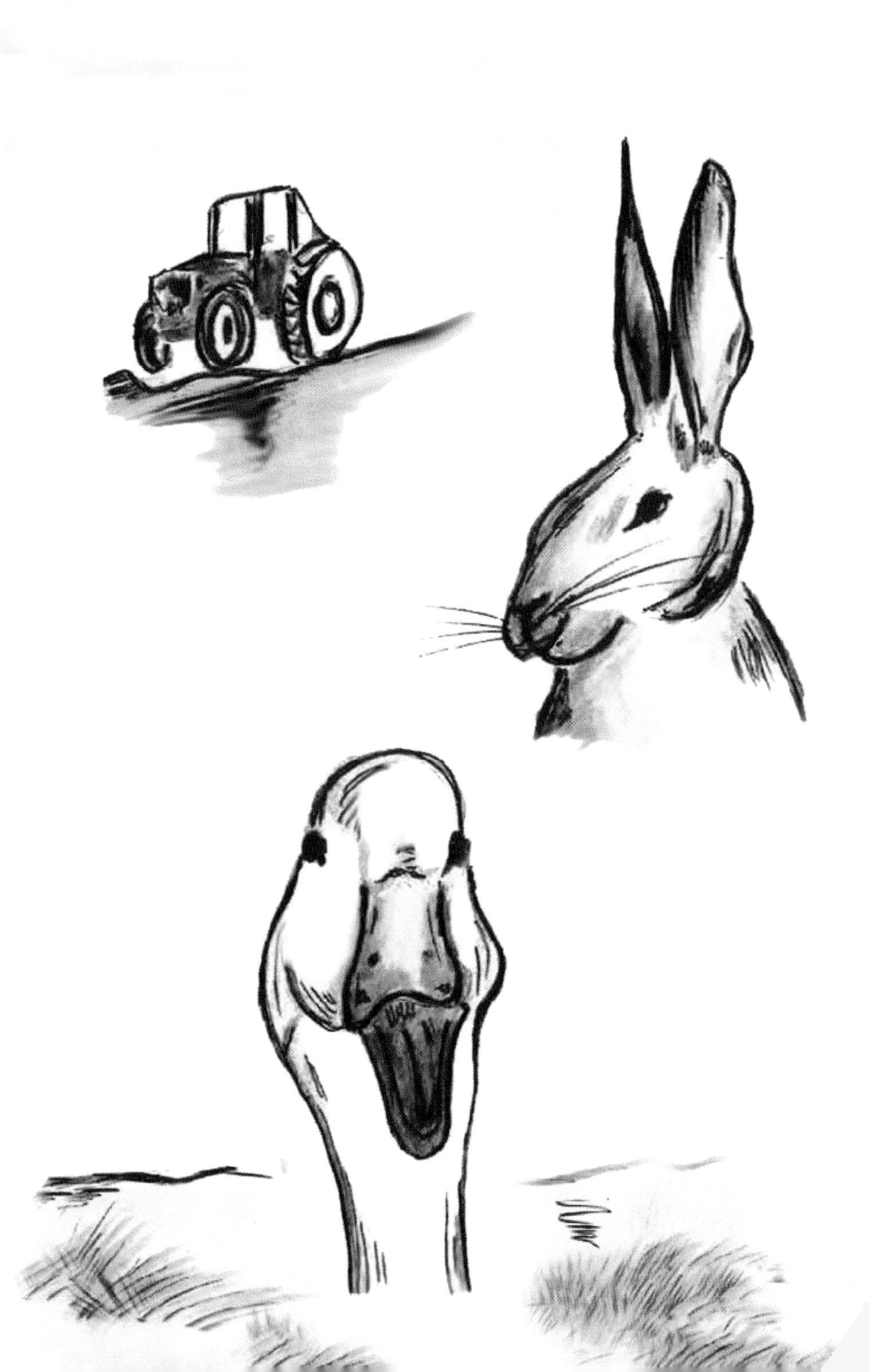

“I’m not duck’s dad
we’re not the same.
We have different beaks
and a different name.”

Duck was wandering,
around the farm.
He came across hare,
at the back of the barn.

“You must be rabbit’s brother
how do you do?”
“Im not rabbit’s brother
and who are you?”

“My name is duck,
I live by that tree
and I have to say,
you look like a rabbit to me.”

“You look like my friend goose,
we have such a bond.
You must have seen him,
he lives by the pond.”

The rabbit and duck,
were sharing some food.
“I met a hare today,
he looked just like you.”

Rabbit laughed;
“We have different legs.
I met a goose,
and you both come from eggs.”

“No no no, how can you say
that I look like a goose?
NO NO ... NO WAY”

The goose and the hare,
they played in the mud.
"I saw a rabbit today,
he looked like you bud."

"How can you say that,
their legs are smaller.
But you look like a duck,
only you are much taller."

One day it rained,
all day on the farm.
And all of the animals,
went into the barn.

The goose and duck waddled,
the rabbit and hare ran.
And on that day,
their friendship began.

The duck, the rabbit,
the goose and the hare.
Are the best of friends,
on a farm
in the country somewhere.

And so if you see animals,
find out their name.
Some are quite similar,
but never the same.

ZOO

A zebra
is not just a stripy horse.
A billy goat,
is not type of sheep of course.

A cat is a cat
and different from others.
And dogs are not
all sisters and brothers.

Printed in Great Britain
by Amazon